MAE AMONG THE STARS

Mae Among the Stars

Copyright © 2018 by Roda Ahmed Hermansen

All rights reserved. Printed in the United States of America.

No part of this book may be used or reproduced in any manner whatsoever without written permission
except in the case of brief quotations embodied in critical articles and reviews. For information address
HarperCollins Children's Books, a division of HarperCollins Publishers, 195 Broadway, New York, NY 10007.

www.harpercollinschildrens.com

ISBN 978-0-06-265173-0

The artist used ink and Adobe Photoshop to create the digital illustrations for this book.

Typography by Chelsea C. Donaldson

21   PC   15

❖

First Edition

To Idil, Isak, and Tor— R.A.

To Archer and Luka— S.B.

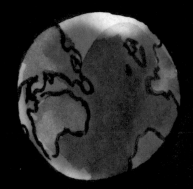

MAE AMONG THE STARS

Written by Roda Ahmed

Illustrations by Stasia Burrington

HARPER

An Imprint of HarperCollinsPublishers

Little Mae was a dreamer.

They say that daydreamers never succeed, but little Mae was different.

One day, Mae was working on an assignment for school

about what she wanted to be when she grew up.

"What will you tell them, Mae?"

"I will tell them I want to see Earth."

"This *is* Earth, Mae," her mother said. "The flowers, the grass, the forest, and the mountains. We live on Earth."

"I know. But I want to see Earth from out there."

"That's an amazing plan, little Mae. Then you have to become

an astronaut—that way you can see Earth from space."

"Astronaut? Do you think I could do that?"

"Of course you can. If you can dream it, if you believe it and work hard for it, anything is possible."

Mae asked her mom to take her to the library. She searched for books about space and astronauts.

After dinner, Mae drew pictures of space, and she even made her own astronaut costume out of old orange curtains and cardboard boxes.

Later she asked her dad, "But how do I become an astronaut?

It seems impossible."

"You will find your way, Mae. Because if you dream it, believe

in it, and work hard for it, anything is possible."

"But space is so, so, so far away!"

"It's closer than you think, little Mae. And you
may get there sooner than you think."

That night, Mae had a happy dream. She was dancing

in space, surrounded by billions of sparkling stars. Below

her she could see Earth floating and turning like a shining

crystal ball.

The next morning, Mae told her parents

about her dream.

She wanted to tell everyone.

And every time she

talked about it,

her eyes would light up.

In the classroom, Miss Bell told everyone to stand in a line on the rug.

"Today, we are all going to share our dreams about the future. What

do you want to be and what do you want to do when you grow up?

Who wants to go first?"

I want to be a firefighter.

All the kids started laughing.

Miss Bell asked, "Mae, are you sure you don't want to be a nurse? Nursing would be a good profession for someone like you."

"I don't want to be a nurse. I want to be an astronaut."

Mae felt very disappointed.

On her way home from school, Mae was quiet.

She looked out the car window. Her world turned

blue and cold; nothing was the way it used to be.

At home, Mae started crying.

"Miss Bell said I can't become an astronaut."

"What a silly thing to say," said her mother.

"She told me I should be a nurse instead," said Mae.

Her mom wiped away her tears. "My dear Mae, I hope you didn't believe her."

"Of course I believed her—she's my teacher!"

"I'm sorry Miss Bell didn't encourage you, but she can't stop you. No one can stop you. Follow your dream, Mae, and go to space."

"Thank you, Mom. I promise when I get to space, I will wave to you and Dad from the spaceship."

Her mom took her hand and they started dancing.

"You must always repeat to yourself: If I can dream it, if I can believe in it, and if I work hard for it, anything is possible."

Mae went on dreaming, believing, and working really hard.

And guess what—

She went to space and waved to her mom and dad on Earth.

Dr. Mae Jemison

Mae Carol Jemison was born October 17, 1956, in Decatur, Alabama. Mae always loved science; she loved being outside and looking up at the stars, knowing that one day she would travel to space.

Mae is highly educated: She graduated from Morgan Park High School in 1973, and at the incredible age of sixteen she enrolled at Stanford University, earning a bachelor of science degree in chemical engineering in 1977. After Mae got her MD in 1981 from Cornell Medical College, she briefly worked as a general practitioner before leaving to work with the Peace Corps as a medical officer in Liberia and Sierra Leone.

When she returned home, Mae decided to follow her childhood dream of going to space, and she accomplished many *firsts*. She applied to NASA's astronaut training program and on June 4, 1987, was accepted. She became the *first* African American female astronaut. On September 12, 1992, Mae's dream finally came true when she traveled to space on the shuttle *Endeavour*, mission STS-47. It was then that Mae officially became the *first* African American woman in space. Mae left NASA in 1993 and became the *first* real astronaut to act in an episode of *Star Trek: The Next Generation*. Today, she heads the Jemison Group and the Dorothy Jemison Foundation for Excellence. Mae speaks fluent Russian, Japanese, and Swahili.